Her Pastry Shifters

Mia Harlan

This book is a work of fiction. All names, characters, places, and incidents are the products of the author's imagination. Any resemblance to actual events, locales, or actual persons, living or dead, is entirely coincidental.

Editing: Kaye Kemp Book Polishing

Proofreading: Pair of Nines Publishing

10 9 8 7 6 5 4 3 2 1

Chapter 1

Jessy

"We're coming to you live from The Epic Bake-Off, where the best pastry chefs compete to see who will hold the title of Most Epic Baker," the show's host announces from the big screen.

She's tall, skinny, and looks like she hasn't tasted a pastry in a very long time. Maybe she's one of those mythical creatures who can eat anything she wants and not gain a single pound. Kind of wish that was me.

A few people in the hotel lobby cheer—they must be here for the Bake-Off, like me—and the three hot-as-sin men in line before me clap. Do they bake? Or are they fans? If they're also mythical creatures who can eat all the dessert they want, I think I might cry.

I'm staring at them as intently as I would at a mouthwatering soufflé baking in the oven. I can't help it. My God, they're delicious. I'm drooling over them almost as much as I'd drool over a buttery, flaky pastry. And, I'm proud to say, mine are so scrumptious that I'm a contestant on the show.

Of course, none of the hotties have so much as looked my way since I got in line behind them. But I'm used to blending into the background. No one ever notices the short, curvy girl unless she's handing them their pastries. But anyone who's tasted what I bake doesn't overlook me twice. Hey, maybe I should shove a Danish or two in their mouths.

"Next," a receptionist calls out.

There are two staff members working the desk, and almost as soon as the three hot men step forward, the other receptionist calls for the next person in line.

"I'd like to check in, please." I slide my credit card and ID across the desk.

"Do you have a reservation?"

I nod.

She smiles and turns to her computer screen. But then her smile falls. "I'm sorry, ma'am. We've been trying to reach you all day. Unfortunately, your room had a plumbing issue, and we're all booked up because of the Bake-Off, so we've had to cancel your reservation." She slides a paper across the desk. "Again, I'm so sorry. Please accept this free one-week stay as an apology. It's valid any time *after* the Bake-Off."

I gawk at the paper, my heart rate skyrocketing. "But I'm one of the contestants. The Bake-Off is why I'm here!" My voice is laced with panic and quite a bit louder than I'd intended.

I glance over my shoulder and notice that people are staring, including one of the men who was in line in front of me. He's tall, tanned, muscular, and has stubble on his cheeks, like he didn't have time to shave this morning. If he had to be at the airport as early as I did, that's probably what happened.

When our eyes meet, my heart skips a beat. Then it skips another ten when I realize just how screwed I am.

"I'm halfway across the country"—I turn to the receptionist, my tone low and pleading—"for the most important competition of my career. What am I supposed to do?"

"I really wish I could help. I'm so, so sorry." She hands me a brown envelope. "These are your competition documents."

"But all the Airbnbs and motels are fully booked. This was the only hotel that had an opening, and now you're telling me I don't have a room?"

"If there was anything else I could do, or any other rooms—"

"Do you have a couch in your break room? A closet? Anything?" My voice turns hysterical, but this is my dream, and it's turning into a nightmare.

"We have room." The deep, sexy voice sends shivers traveling down my spine, and a wave of hope courses through me.

"You do?" I turn to stare at the three men who were in line in front of me.

The one I made eye contact with earlier gives me a small smile. "I said we have room," he repeats. "We booked a suite. And we'd be happy to double up so you can have one of the beds. We're here for the competition, too."

He opens a brown envelope and takes out three badges.

My heart starts to race. The thought of sharing a room with them makes me flush. I'm surprised I don't turn into a puddle at their feet.

I stare, wide-eyed, at his equally wide-eyed friends. They look like they'd been shocked into complete silence. They're probably thinking of a polite way to tell him he's nuts and they're not okay sharing their space with a curvy baker they just met.

"Look, I don't want to inconvenience your friends," I tell him, because it's the right thing to do. Even if I am desperate, and I have no clue what I'll do if they say no.

Chapter 2

Mac

"It wouldn't be an inconvenience," I tell the breathtaking, voluptuous beauty.

She's wearing black yoga pants that hug her sweet curves, simple sneakers, and a t-shirt that says 'Life is what you bake it.' A woman after my own heart. But her eyes are full of apprehension, which means I'm going to need backup.

"We don't mind sharing. Right, guys?"

I shoot my two best friends-turned-business partners a look that says I will end you if you disagree. But I needn't have worried. One look at them tells me they're on board. And I know them well enough to recognize that, more likely than not, our soon-to-be roommate is their fated mate, too. So 'sharing' just took on a whole new meaning.

I want to pull our baker into my arms and tell her everything will be okay. That I'll take care of it, and her, for the rest of her life. But I'm more likely to scare her off than comfort her, so I force myself to stay put.

"We don't mind." Bax shoots her the same friendly smile that always works on the customers. It seems to put her at ease.

Rune crosses his tattooed arms in front of his muscular chest. Baking is hard physical labor; don't let anyone tell you otherwise. We hand-make everything. Literally. We have no machines except for an oven in our shop. Between whisking gallons of cream, kneading dough, and stocking heavy bags of flour and sugar, all three of us are in great shape. Though, of course, our shifter powers play a big role in that.

"Rune?" I nudge the man.

He clears his throat. And clears his throat again. Then nods. He's never been a man of many words, and sometimes forcing him to talk makes him accidentally shift—which would make me shift, too—so it's better if he stays silent.

"If you really don't mind," our curvy baker says with a small smile. "I'm Jessy."

"Luke MacMaster," I tell her. "But I just go by Mac."

"Baxter Carlton," Bax says. "Go by Car professionally, but I'm Bax to my friends." He extends his hand. "I know we're competing against each other, but I hope we can be friends, Jessy."

"Of course." She smiles and slips her small hand into his much larger one.

Never thought I'd envy a simple handshake, but here I am. If I hadn't been so focused on putting her at ease, I would have thought to shake her hand. Now, it's too late. Who knows how long it'll be before I finally get to touch her? So I go all in and awkwardly shove my hand out anyway.

Chapter 3

Jessy

My cheeks flush as I shake hands with Mac and turn to the third man, who's been silently watching me from beneath hooded eyelids. "You're Rune, right?"

He grunts and nods.

I don't know how he manages it, but he makes me melt with a single look. All three of them do.

"I'll grab your bag," Bax says.

Rune grunts, beats him to it, and scoops it under his arm.

"I can get someone to help with that," the receptionist tells him.

He pointedly ignores her.

"I'm sure it weighs less than a bag of flour," Mac says.

"I guess." My cheeks flush.

Rune nods and, without a word, heads toward the elevators.

"I'm so glad everything worked out, ma'am," the receptionist says, slyly casting looks at the guys. They are hot. "Don't forget these."

She hands me the envelope, my one-week stay voucher, and my credit card and ID. I slip everything into the envelope, then Mac places a hand on the small of my back and guides me after Rune.

I stumble. His touch has the same effect on me as shaking his and Bax's hands. For a second, I forget how to breathe. And when the four of us all squeeze into an elevator, with Rune behind me, Mac on my left, and Bax on my right, I struggle not to hyperventilate at all the steamy elevator scenes flooding through my mind right now. Or tremble like the hot mess that I am. A hot mess who hasn't had a man between her legs in way too long and is now picturing herself with three.

Three? Ugh, what's wrong with you, Jessy? I ask myself.

The guys are being so nice, giving me a place to stay. I can't just spend the whole competition drooling over them like a lovesick puppy. I'll just end up making them regret coming to my rescue. Especially when there's no way they're into me. No one's ever into the curvy girl who's only interested in baking and eating pastries.

Chapter 4

Bax

"So, Bax." The moment my name slips past her kissable lips, my cock stands at attention. It's as hard as a rolling pin and just as wide, too. I bet it would fit in that mouth of hers.

"Yes, Jessy?" I say her name just for an excuse to taste it again. It sounds so right on my lips. Just like she's so right for me.

My fated mate, and she doesn't even know it yet.

Fuck.

Mac told me about those before I came to Shifter Bay. And after I shifted for the first time, and the town welcomed me with open arms, I heard plenty of stories about true love that's meant to be.

I'd never imagined that a guy like me, born human, would ever have one... But I'd hoped. I'd dreamed. But I didn't actually expect it to happen. Except it did, and Jessy's real. She's here, and she's fated to be with me... and with my two best friends. I'm almost positive they feel the same way about her as I do, and that is going to take a bit longer getting used to. Being born human, I'm not into sharing all that much, but if I have to share with anyone, these are the guys I'd trust with my life. And hers, too.

"What were you going to ask, Jessy?" I love saying her name. I want to say it while I'm buried deep inside her... and there goes another twitch from my rolling pin cock. This might be a problem.

"Why do you go by Car professionally? If you don't mind my asking. You are a baker, aren't you? Not a mechanic?"

"I am." I force myself to keep my tone light. Friendly. *Get down, you useless appendage! Nothing is happening right now!*

Her question doesn't bother me. The fact that she's stringing together full sentences while I'm picturing all the places I'd like to fuck her does.

Shit.

What if she doesn't feel the pull between us? What if it takes her time? What if she never accepts all three of us as her fated mates and wants to date one man the way most people do?

Most humans are monogamous, unlike shifters. But what if she's happy being the former? What if... What if...she only takes one of us and rejects the rest? I turn away from her and focus on taking slow, deep breaths before I accidentally shift.

Chapter 5

Jessy

"I'm so sorry. I didn't mean to offend you." I flush, watching him cross his muscular arms in front of his broad chest. "I was just curious why you go by Car, that's all. You obviously don't have to tell me!"

The elevator dings, the door opens on the ninth floor, and Bax races out like he can't get away from me fast enough.

This is awful. I've literally only known these guys for two minutes, and they're probably going to kick me out of their suite and tell me this isn't going to work.

"He's not offended," Mac says. "He's just nervous."

"Nervous? Why?"

"The competition," Bax blurts out and starts to blush. Unlike Mac, he's clean shaven, which makes his embarrassment even more obvious. "Macaroon."

"You're nervous about making a macaroon?" I ask in surprise. "I'll be happy to—"

Mac lets out a bark of laughter.

"What?" I ask, because it's obvious I missed something.

"MacCarRune is the name of our bakery," Mac says proudly.

"Oh." I flush. I should have figured it out. Instead, I was too busy drooling over the three men to pick up on it. So now I'm just the idiot who offered him help with his macaroons.

Maybe I should just give up on this contest and fly back home. The universe clearly doesn't want me to win, and I've already managed to piss off one guy, while the other two probably think I'm an idiot.

Chapter 6

Rune

I know when someone needs to be alone. I recognize it because it happens to me.

I'm not good around people. I prefer pastries.

My fated mate is better with people than I am, but as much as she's trying to hide it, I can tell she wants to run. Probably would have, if I wasn't holding her suitcase hostage, and we weren't her only ticket to a place to stay.

"Come." I wrap my free hand around hers and pull her down the hall, enjoying the feeling of her soft skin.

To my surprise, she doesn't protest or ask where we're going.

I scan the room numbers, and when I spot ours, I let go of her hand long enough to grab my key card from my pocket.

I swipe it, pull her into the suite, and lead her down the hall to the nearest bedroom.

"Rune?" She sounds as breathless as I feel.

I don't reply. I can't. When I try, my throat clogs up.

I lead her inside the room, set her suitcase down by the bed, and turn to leave.

"Yours," I throw over my shoulder and get the hell out of there before I lose all self-control.

"What happened?" Mac scowls when I return to the living room.

He and Bax stare after her like I've just told them they're not allowed to eat any pastries for a week and then proceeded to eat a cherry cheese Danish in front of them.

"She needed space." I glance back at the room where I left her, but the door remains closed. I don't think she's coming out anytime soon.

"Fuck." Bax heads into the in-suite kitchen and gestures for us to follow. "I was worried about that."

"Is she your fated mate?" Mac asks him.

Bax nods.

"Mine, too," I add.

"And mine," Mac says.

We stare at each other. It's a comfortable silence, one born of years of baking side by side. We don't need words to communicate, just time to accept the fact that the decadent baker belongs to all three of us, and that's just the way it's going to be.

"We need to come up with a plan," Mac says.

I nod. “Do we tell her we’re shifters and she’s ours before we—” I’m about to say ‘claim her,’ but I guess I’ve already strung too many words in a row, because I croissant onto the floor.

And I guess I have my answer when she gasps from the doorway.

Chapter 7

Jessy

I gape at the delicious-looking croissant on the kitchen floor. If I saw it in a bakery, I'd order it in a heartbeat—and savor every bite. But where did it come from? And where is Rune? And why is this delicious pastry on the floor?

I look around, but there's no sign of him. And then Mac disappears. I yelp. An eclair materializes in his place, and I alternate between drooling over how delicious it looks and freaking out because I'm clearly hallucinating.

"Oh, shit. Oh, shit. Oh, shit," Bax mutters under his breath. He stares at me with wide, panicked eyes, and then he goes poof. In his place, a cannoli.

I stumble back. "This isn't happening. It's a dream. A very weird, very delicious dream where hot men turn into desserts." I pinch myself and gasp. It hurts. "Did I accidentally eat a special brownie?"

Suddenly, the croissant disappears. Rune reappears, looking exactly the same... almost like he'd always been there. "It's not a dream, and you're not hallucinating," he says. "We're Bayans."

Mac reappears next to him.

“And we shift into p—” Rune disappears again.

Then Mac disappears, but the croissant and eclair are back. And there’s still no sign of Bax, just the delicious-looking cannoli.

This is normal. Everything is normal.

I pinch myself again. Still hurts. I’ve definitely lost it.

“Bayans,” I repeat as I process everything I just saw. “Are you saying you’re... pastry *shifters*? Like wolf and bear and dragon shifters, but *pastries?*”

“Exactly,” Rune says when he reappears. He doesn’t explain further. He just nods.

“You know about shifters?” Mac asks as he reappears next to him.

“From books.” My cheeks flush, because I like my books dirty—and I want to see these shifters hard and very, very naked. “Wait, are you saying wolf shifters are real? And bears?”

“And dragons.” Mac nods, turning my entire world upside down. “We’re a little different, though. We’re from a small town called Shifter Bay, where everyone shifts into objects—like pastries, but other things too. Like, a block of ice, a rubber duckie, a donut, a paperback novel, you name it.”

I’d think he was messing with me if I hadn’t seen it for myself.

"We also can't always control when we shift. Rune shifts if he says too much all at once—so he tends to stay quiet. Though he was a man of few words before he became a shifter, too."

"So you weren't always a shifter?" I ask Rune.

He shakes his head.

"I'm a sympathetic shifter," Mac says. "If Rune shifts, I'll shift too. So it's better if I talk for him. At least for now."

"What about Bax?" I ask, even though I feel like I'm in some alternate reality where guys shift into my favorite thing in the whole wide world: baked goods.

"He shifts when he's anxious." Mac says as Bax reappears next to him. "What else would you like to know?"

I have so many questions I don't even know where to start. But at the top of my list is whether I'm high.

Chapter 8

Bax

Things seem to be going relatively well.

Jessy isn't running out of the kitchen screaming. She's not freaking out on us, either. And she reads books about shifters. That has to be a good sign. Not that anyone knows about us Bayans.

"Jessy..." Fuck. I think I'm going to spend the rest of my life just saying her name. "I know how weird this must be. When I first found out Mac was a pastry shifter... Let's just say you're handling this a lot better than I did."

"He thought I'd drugged him." Mac grins. "And when Rune found out, he didn't speak to me for two days. Then he came up to me and said 'okay.'"

"Okay?" Jessy gives him an amused smile I wish was aimed at me.

Rune shrugs.

"I'd think I was drugged, too, but all I had was that brownie on the flight." Jessy turns to me. "I'm still half-convinced I'm dreaming. I mean, pastry shifters?"

"I know it's not as glamorous as a wolf or bear shifter or whatever." I rub the back of my neck. "But it has its perks."

"Not as glamorous? Are you kidding me?" She gapes at me. "I love pastries. They are my favorite thing in the entire world. I'm a baker! Wolves and bears… I could do with or without, but baked goods are my life." She shrugs. "Do you have any shifter powers? Like super strength or night vision or whatever?"

"Nothing like that. But we can eat as many pastries as we want without feeling full or gaining weight."

"Wait, what? You're kidding me, right?" Her eyes grow wide.

"Nope." I shake my head. "Magic."

"Unlimited cannoli?"

I nod.

"And eclairs?"

Mac nods.

"And croissants?"

Rune nods.

"Then sign me up."

"What?" This time it's my turn to gape at her.

"How do I become one?" she demands. "I want to shift into a pastry and eat all the pastries I want." She cups her rounded stomach, and her cheeks flush. "I could stand to lose a few pounds. More than a few."

"No." I shake my head, completely horrified at the thought, and her face falls. "Jessy, you look perfect just the way you are."

Mac and Rune nod in agreement.

"Oh, come on." She rolls her eyes.

"I'm serious," I tell her. "Being a pastry shifter wouldn't change how you look. And I wouldn't want it to."

"You're sexy as hell, Jessy," Rune adds. "You don't need to lose—"

He shifts. Bam. Croissant. Mac follows suit.

"Jessy, I..." It's up to me to convince her that she's the most stunning woman I've ever met. Especially when I'm the one who mentioned weight gain and made her self-conscious in the first place.

She looks at me with wide, expectant eyes.

"I..." I say the first thing that comes to mind, "want to fuck you."

And then, bam, cannoli.

Chapter 9

Jessy

Hot guy Bax wants to fuck me? Hell, yes.

I've been wet practically since the first moment I met these guys, and I'm not passing the opportunity with Bax up. Just one problem: I can't grab him and drag him to the bedroom, because he's a cannoli.

I could carry him to the bedroom, though.

I pick up the cannoli and take two steps. He shifts in my arms, and we both collapse to the kitchen floor.

"I'm so, so—" Bax shifts back into a cannoli.

Mac, who'd shifted back a second ago, shifts into an eclair. Which just leaves Rune and me in human form. He raises an eyebrow, and I flush scarlet. I'm the girl who just tried to carry a cannoli off to her bedroom because she's horny. How embarrassing is that?

My flush deepens.

"Have silent sex with me?" Rune asks.

"What?" I gape at him. I'm not sure what throws me more, the fact that the guy asked for silent sex or that a hottie like him would want to hook up with me. Oh, or the fact that the guys keep shifting into pastries.

"If I talk..." Rune points at the cannoli and eclair currently on the floor.

Oh, right. He shifts if he says more than, like, ten words.

He crooks his finger at me, gesturing for me to come to him.

My heart pounds wildly in my chest. I want this. I want him. I—

A knock at the door interrupts us.

"Just ignore—" Rune starts to say, and then he shifts.

Bam. Croissant.

Chapter 10

Mac

Fucking hell.

I grew up in Shifter Bay. I'm used to people shifting at inopportune moments. But we're botching this up, big time. Unless I can get Rune's talking and Bax's anxiety under control, I'll be spending my time with my mate as an eclair instead of fucking her with my eclair. And I don't mean the one I shift into.

My cock. I mean my cock.

"I guess I'll get the door, then," Jessy tells our shifted forms.

Internally, I sigh. Externally, I'm stuck on the floor because I'm a fucking eclair. Which has never bothered me before—they've always been my favorite pastries. Delicious, chocolaty, creamy goodness.

From my vantage point on the kitchen floor, I watch Jessy's round, black yoga pant-clad bottom sway as she heads to the door. I could watch those sweet curves of hers all day—though I'd rather run my hands all over that sweet body of hers.

“Who is it?” Jessy asks.

“Room service,” a man calls from the other side of the door.

Jessy opens it, and he wheels a cart inside the room. “We’ve got an assortment of baked goods prcpared by last year’s winner for all our contestants... Oh, I didn’t see you there,” he adds as Bax shifts back.

Rune follows. I shift back last.

“Where did you all come from?” The confused hotel employee gapes at us.

“The kitchen,” I tell him. “Thank you for the dessert.”

I hand him a twenty-dollar bill and quickly guide him out of the room. Once he’s gone, I turn to Rune. “Don’t talk.”

Rune salutes me and winks at Jessy.

I squeeze Bax’s shoulder so he knows I’ve got his back. He nods to tell me he’s no longer feeling anxious.

“Good.” Because I was three seconds from shoving half the baked goods in his mouth to calm him. Instead, I turn to Jessy and blurt, “There’s one last thing you need to know. You’re our fated mate.”

Chapter 11

Jessy

"I'm your *fated mate*? That's a real thing?" I demand, forgetting all about the cart of pastries.

"It is," Bax tells me. "And you're mine, Jessy."

"And mine," Mac adds.

"And mine," Rune finishes.

"You guys are just messing with me," I say. They must be, right? There's no way any of this is real. Being fated to be with a bunch of pastries... then again, it sort of makes sense. Baking is my life—and it's theirs too. Plus, I've been drawn to these men from the first moment I saw them.

"We'd never lie to you, Jessy," Bax says.

"I swear it's all true," Mac says.

Rune nods.

And deep down, I know I can trust them. "So let me get this straight... I have *three* fated mates. They're the hottest men I've ever met. And they shift into my favorite thing in the whole world?"

Bax breaks into a grin. "You think we're hot?"

"The hottest men she's ever seen," Mac says with a huge smile.

My cheeks flush.

Rune grabs my waist, pulls me into his hard chest, and covers my lips with his.

The croissant shifter is a man of few words, but he sure knows how to use his mouth. He claims my lips in a searing kiss that I feel all the way to my toes and kisses the living daylights out of me.

Chapter 12

Rune

Sometimes, talking is overrated. In my case, it also sends me to Croissant City—but that's besides the point.

Right now, I plan to show my mate how much I want her, and I don't need words for that.

I slide my tongue into her mouth and back her up until we reach the dessert cart. I blindly reach for something—which ends up being a bite-sized chocolate cake—and break the kiss long enough to take a bite and offer the other half to my mate. Who can resist the delicious promise of baked goods?

"Mmmm." She lets out a moan I feel straight down to my balls. And I decide I'll do whatever it takes to make her moan like that. Again. And again. Ideally naked, with my tongue against her delectable pussy. "The salt really brings out the flavor."

She's talking about the chocolate cake, and she's right. That, and the fact that she's a baker, too, makes my blood boil with need.

I cup the back of her head and pull her in for a kiss. She tastes delicious, like salt, chocolate, and something that is purely Jessy.

She wraps her arms around my neck, and I cup her hot, round ass. I lift her easily—I'm a baker, after all—and cross the living room to the brown leather couch.

I set my girl down without breaking the kiss. She sinks into the couch, and I kneel in front of her and slowly run my hands up her inner thighs.

"Room for two more?" Mac asks as he and Bax settle on the couch on either side of her.

I break our kiss to make sure our girl is okay, and grin when I realize my friends are each holding a plate of pastries. They really know what's what.

Chapter 13

Jessy

"Whoa," I breathe as I look at the pastries and the three hot guys surrounding me. "The only thing that would make this moment better is if you were all naked."

Bax smirks and hands me his plate of pastries. "That can be arranged."

I drool over the delicious desserts and the even more delicious chest he reveals as he peels off his shirt. Bax is made of lean, hard muscle—which makes sense since the guy has unlimited pastry metabolism. Lucky guy.

Rune strips next. His shoulders are broader than Bax's, and he's got the large, bulging muscles of a man who isn't afraid of hard work. Rolling dough and lifting bags of flour and sugar is no joke.

Rune is also covered in tattoos. I lean forward and run my fingers over the croissant and the date printed underneath.

"First shift," he says gruffly.

He doesn't say more. I don't ask him to. I want him nice and hard, not soft and fluffy. And there are plenty of other fluffy pastries on the plate Bax just handed me.

I'm examining the selection when Mac pulls off his own shirt, and my gaze is drawn to him. Or, more specifically, his abs.

"Holy crap, I want to lick icing off those abs." *Shit, did I just say that out loud?*

Apparently, I did, because Mac grins. "Only if I can lick it off every part of you."

I resist the urge to fan myself. "Deal."

Chapter 14

Mac

Deal.

For a second, my brain short circuits. I finally get to touch my Jessy. Not just touch. Lick. Suck.

Fuck.

And then it sinks in, and I jump into action.

I shove my plate of pastries at Rune. I take Jessy's plate and practically throw it at Bax.

Then I reach for the hem of her shirt. "Can I take this off?"

"Please," she says breathlessly, which turns me the hell on. Almost as much as the fact that she wants to lick icing off me.

I'm pretty sure that whatever I bake from now on will have icing, and all I'll be able to think of is how it'll taste when I eat it off her.

I peel off her shirt and pull her in for a kiss. "Mmm, chocolate."

I run my hands up and down her arms, her sides, the tops of her breasts.

She gasps and takes off her bra. Thank the pastries in heaven.

I spot the cupcake sitting in the middle of Bax's plate and just go for it, smashing it onto Jessy's bare breast.

She gasps, but I can't tell if it's pleasure or surprise.

"Don't worry, baby, I'll clean you up," I tell her and get to work with my tongue.

I suck her sweet, delicious nipple into my mouth. She moans. I swirl my tongue around, collecting errant icing, and she arches her back, encouraging me. Fuck, she's hot.

I groan. "You're the best dessert I've ever had. And I'm a baker, Jessy. That says a lot."

Chapter 15

Jessy

"That's so..." I moan. "Sweet. No pun intended. Seriously, Mac. No one's ever said that to me before."

"We'll have to remedy that." Mac gives my nipple another lick.

Pleasure courses through me. I arch my hips slightly, needing more, and Rune slides his hands up my inner thighs. I moan.

"Lift," he orders, and when I raise my hips, he pulls my yoga pants off, taking my panties with them.

The couch is cold against my bare ass, but I barely have a second to think about that before I feel something wet and sticky on my inner thigh.

Mac's head blocks my view, but it doesn't feel like icing. Maybe jelly?

He licks it off, then adds more filling higher up, closer to my core.

"More," I whimper.

Bax grabs a cannoli, sticks his finger deep into the filling, and runs it along my lips. I moan as I taste the slightly sweet, creamy ricotta.

"Wait," I say. All three guys freeze. "That's a cannoli."

Bax nods.

"And you're a cannoli."

He nods again.

"Does that mean you have sex in cannoli form?" I ask, slightly horrified at the mental image.

"No." Bax snorts. "You read books about shifters, right?"

"All the time."

"And do wolf shifters have sex with humans while they're in wolf form?"

I shake my head.

"How about bear shifters?"

I shake my head again. "In the books I read, they definitely don't… and I wouldn't want them to."

Mac snorts. "How would you even have sex with a pastry? I mean, other than like this." He licks the icing off my nipple.

"Or this." Bax slides his index finger into my mouth. It's covered in ricotta, and it's delicious.

“Or… this.” Rune spreads more of the cherry cheese Danish filling on my inner thighs, moving closer and closer to my core.

“How does it taste?” Bax asks.

It takes me a second to realize he’s talking to me.

“Amazing,” I moan.

Rune chuckles between my thighs. “It’s about to get a whole lot b—”

Chapter 16

Rune

Fuck, I should have known better than to talk so much.

Jessy's thighs are spread wide, inviting me to lick her core, and what am I doing? Lying on the carpeted floor in croissant form while Mac is lying next to her in eclair form.

Shift back, shift back, shift back, I repeat over and over again as Jessy moans. I swore I'd make her moan like that, but I decided to be all talk and no action, so here I am.

Luckily, we share our fated mate with Bax, and he keeps her busy and wet. He slides a finger covered in cannoli filling past her tempting pink lips. Meanwhile, I'm tempted by her other set of lips.

The moment I shift back, I pounce. I don't waste another second teasing her. I dive between her legs and suck her clit into my mouth.

Jessy's hips fly off the couch. She lets out a cry that's muffled by Bax's finger, followed by whimper after whimper as I lick and suck.

Fuck, I love hearing those sounds coming from my mate, but I need more. I want to make her come.

I lick my index and middle finger, making sure to get any stray icing, before I slide them inside her. I start to fuck her with my fingers the way I wish I was doing with my cock.

Jessy gasps. She pumps her hips, urging me on, and cries out when I start teasing her clit with my tongue.

"Suck on this," Bax says. It sounds so fucking dirty, but he offers her his fingers, which are covered in more cannoli filling.

Mac tugs on one of Jessy's nipples while he licks the other, and our girl goes wild.

She arches into his touch. She moans around Bax's fingers. And her hips start to tremble as she clenches around my fingers and starts to come.

Chapter 17

Jessy

I think I just died and went to heaven. No, I'm sure I have.

Because three of the hottest bakers I've ever met just gave me the best orgasm of my life.

I'm still trembling when Rune scoops me up in his arms and carries me into one of the bedrooms. He drops me in the middle of the king-sized bed and pulls down his pants.

Multiple tattoos wind down his thighs, but I can't seem to look past his cock long enough to take in details. His erection stands long and proud against his hard, tattooed abs. His tip just reaches the croissant—I wonder if that was intentional.

He strokes himself, and just like that, I'm wet and ready again. Oh, who am I kidding? I've been ready since two seconds after I had that orgasm. How can I not be when I have three hot men—and their cocks—standing at attention for me?

Bax and Mac have pulled their pants off, too, and I'm shocked that they all want me. But you can't argue with erections. Especially ones that rival the rolling pins in my bakery's kitchen.

Mac slips on a condom and tosses two more on the nightstand. I stare at them for several long seconds.

"Are you having second thoughts?" he asks.

"Hell no. I'm hoping those condoms are a promise."

Bax and Rune share matching grins, while Mac takes his place between my thighs. He positions his cock at my entrance and takes his time—I mean, really takes his time—sliding inside me. I dig my fingers into his buttocks and urge him on.

"I could make croquembouche faster, Mac."

For a split second, I'm worried I've offended him, but he starts to laugh, and a cocky smirk tugs on his lips.

And then he slams inside me, hard and fast. I cry out and dig my fingernails into his back. "You're huge!" I gasp.

He pauses, giving me a moment to adjust before sliding back out and slamming into me again. And he watches my face the entire time, like he's feeding off my every reaction as I meet him thrust for thrust. The pleasure builds like dough expanding in an oven, and then I explode, Mac's name on my lips.

Chapter 18

Jessy

"So, what happens next?" I ask as I lie, sated, in the middle of the king-sized bed.

"Round two?" Mac teases.

"You mean with the competition?" Bax asks.

"Oh, shit. The competition!" I bolt up in bed. "We have to be at the opening ceremony at seven. What time is it?"

Mac chuckles. "Don't worry. We've got time."

"Is it going to be weird?" I ask, cheeks flushed. "Competing against each other, I mean?"

Rune tucks a strand of hair behind my ear. "We could always team up."

I picture him standing behind me, helping me knead dough, his hard cock pressed against my ass, and shake my head. "I don't think I'd be able to focus. We'd never win, and we might end up naked on TV."

"We don't really care about that," Bax says. "We only agreed to be here because we love baking. And the competition is going to give our bakery great exposure, no matter where we place."

"Then I won't feel bad when I crush you."

All three guys gape at me.

I snort. "What? I'm a little competitive."

"A little?" Bax rolls on top of me. He's already hard, and his cock nudges my entrance.

I moan. "Okay, a lot."

"Then I have a game for you," Bax whispers. "I bet I can make you come first."

I gasp as he slams into me and then pulls out. "You're on."

"Wait," Rune says. "When you asked what happens next, did you mean—"

He shifts into a croissant. Mac turns into an eclair. Bax slides in and out of me, setting a slow, teasing pace.

I moan and glance at Rune and Mac. "They can still hear us, right?" I ask.

"And see us." Bax groans as he continues fucking me.

Which is a huge turn on. But I don't like losing, so I clench around Bax to try to make him come first.

He groans. "Jessy, what did you mean before?"

I'm so focused on staving off the pleasure building between my legs, it takes me a few seconds to register his words.

Bax slams into me again, and I gasp. "Mean by what?"

Rune shifts back and starts teasing my nipple. "You asked what happens next."

"Oh." I moan and struggle not to come. "That's not fair. You're cheating."

Bax grins. "It's not cheating when we're a team."

Mac shifts back and nuzzles my neck. "And hopefully, one day, you'll be part of our team," he adds. "I know we just met, but I'm falling for you."

I can't quite believe we're having this conversation while Bax is sliding in and out of me, and all three guys are trying to make me come, but I moan in agreement. "I'm falling for you too. For all of you."

"Good." Bax grins and fucks me harder. "Because I'm yours for as long as you'll have me. Hopefully, forever."

"So am I." Rune sucks my nipple into his mouth.

Mac kisses me, and I shatter. The orgasm rocks through me, and I see stars. Or maybe pastries.

When Mac pulls back, Rune threads a hand through my hair and pulls me in for a slow, luxurious kiss. I melt against his lips, and then he's pulling away and Bax is there, pulling me onto his lap and peppering my face with soft kisses.

When I can finally form coherent sentences again, I let out a satisfied sigh. "You may have won this round, but I plan to win the Bake-Off."

He grins. "Oh, I don't doubt it. But after you do, would you consider coming back with us to Shifter Bay and becoming a shifter like us?"

"Would it mean I would get to shift into a pastry?"

The guys nod.

"And have hot sex with the three of you?"

They nod again.

"And eat unlimited pastries for the rest of my life?"

They grin.

"Then hell, yeah!"

Chapter 19

Jessy

"Welcome back to the Epic Bake-Off! Our judges are busy deliberating over which entry will be the winner tonight, while our two finalists—Baxter Carlton from MacCarRune Bakery and Jessy Alexander from Jessy Bakes—are backstage right now waiting for the results. We'll be calling them out shortly to announce who will take home the fifty thousand dollar prize tonight. But while we wait, let's take a closer look at their creations... and have a little taste." Sienna, the tall, skinny blonde hosting the Epic Bake-Off, picks up a fork and winks at the camera.

"She's some sort of mythical creature," I tell the guys as I stare up at the big screen. "Are you sure she's not a shifter? Or a vampire?" Because apparently those are real, too.

"Pretty sure." Mac tugs me toward him by my apron.

I wrap my arms around his neck and get up on tiptoe to kiss him. When I pull back, my lips tingle.

His gaze is still locked on my mouth when he asks, "Why do you think she's a supe?"

"A soup? You mean people can shift into soup, too? Isn't that rather messy? And what happens if they spill some? Do they, like, lose some of their hair when they shift back?"

Rune snorts.

Bax shakes his head. "Mac meant supe, as in supernatural. Do you know something we don't?"

I shrug. "Obviously, she can't be real. She sampled every entry in the entire competition. That's like a gazillion calories. No one can eat that many desserts and stay that skinny."

"Jessy," Rune growls in warning, sidling up behind me. He nuzzles my neck and runs his hands up and down my curvy hips but doesn't say anything else. He's probably worried that if he talks, he'll accidentally shift.

Bax takes Mac's place in front of me. "Don't tell me our perfect," he kisses me softly, "gorgeous," he cups my ass, "voluptuous," he pulls me into his chest, "mate," he grinds his hips against mine and heat builds between my thighs, "is jealous."

I moan. "Nope. Definitely not jealous."

Bax pulls back to look at me.

"Okay, maybe a little."

"You have nothing to be jealous of," Mac tells me. "You are the most beautiful woman on this earth."

My eyes widen. "Really?" I blurt out.

Mac's face softens. He tucks a stray hair behind my ear. But it is Bax who responds, "Without a doubt, and we are lucky we have the honor of calling you ours."

I glance to Rune, who nods. And just like that, I'm not jealous anymore. I have three hot pastry shifter mates who can't get enough of my curvy body... and fine; I admit it, I'm looking forward to becoming a shifter, too, and eating unlimited desserts without gaining a single pound. Pastry shifter metabolism, here I come!

Bax leans in to kiss me, distracting me from my delicious thoughts with new, different—but equally delicious—thoughts, while Mac and Rune nuzzle my neck. Heat courses through me, and I'm this close to stripping off all our clothes when I remember we're in the backstage lounge. The judges could have the result ready for us at any moment. I do not need to go viral because I found out I won the Epic Bake-Off while butt naked.

Chapter 20

Jessy

"We don't have time," I tell the guys regretfully as I gesture at the big screen.

The camera is zoomed in on the three bakers who will decide the fate of the bake-off, but it looks like they're still busy whispering among themselves while sneaking bites of our cakes, blissful expressions on their faces.

I gasp. "We haven't even tried the cakes."

That seems to get my guys' attention, and we relocate to the cart Sienna wheeled in earlier.

I grab a plate with Bax's creation, a chocolate drip cake, and take a bite. "Wow, this is..." I moan. "Utter perfection. I mean, I'm still going to win, but seriously... Magic in every bite."

"That's because it is magic," Bax reminds me.

"Yeah, I know. Everything you bake turns out perfect." It's no wonder he's been the one doing the baking in the competition.

Bax shakes his head. "Not everything. Obviously, if I tried to make something taste bad, it would. But so long as I put in the right ingredients, the magic gives them an extra oomph of perfection."

"It's hard to compete with perfection." I smirk, "But I still think I won."

All three guys gape at me.

"If anyone could beat me, it's you," Bax says, and I can tell he means it.

"You're an amazing baker. I heard about you before I met you, and we rarely get news about humans," Mac adds, grabbing a plate with my cake.

Rune nods in agreement and grabs a plate with a slice of my entry, a mango cake with a special secret ingredient. One that just might be able to take on Bax's cake.

I may not achieve perfect, but I've got something better—that right amount of weird that will make those judges stop and take notice. Too much weird, and they'll trash my cake... and my reputation. But if I got it just right, they will never forget me.

Rune takes a bite of my cake, and his eyes widen. "Shit, Jessy. This is..." He grabs another forkful. "*Everything*! What's in this? I've never tasted anything—" He strings together one word too many and shifts into a croissant. His plate clatters onto the floor next to him, thankfully face-up, thus salvaging my cake.

Mac promptly shifts into an eclair. His plate stays face-up too, and the slice of cake is missing a bite-sized chunk.

Luckily, the backstage lounge isn't equipped with cameras, so at least the rest of the world isn't about to find out that shifters are real.

I'm surprised Bax managed not to shift while baking, but he only shifts when he's anxious. And apparently he's not the least bit worried about the outcome of the competition. Then again, neither am I.

I may not always be confident about my curves, but give me an apron, and I bring it.

I take another bite of Bax's cake and moan when a knock echoes from the other side of the door. "Is everyone decent? Because we're ready for you."

"Coming." I grab Rune's plate, while Bax grabs Mac's. We set them back on the cart and head toward the door.

Rune shifts back first.

Mac follows suit and catches up to me. "A dash of hot pepper?" he whispers in my ear. "You really like things spicy."

I step out of the lounge, smile at Sienna, and glance back over my shoulder. "I take it you approve?"

Mac nods. "More than approve. Your cake was magical."

"Both cakes were," Sienna gushes to Bax and me as she gestures for us to follow her down the hall. "I don't know how the judges could possibly choose between them."

"I think Jessy's secret ingredient just might do it." Mac's eyes dance. And is it bad that I really want him to be right? I'm competitive, so sue me.

Sienna pretends to zip her lips shut. "You're going to have to wait and see."

She steps into the competition room, but when I move to follow, Bax tugs on my hand. He stops me a second before we step inside. "Jessy, I just want you to know that no matter what happens out there, the only prize I care about is you."

"And we'll share the prize money either way," Mac adds. We'd agreed on that before the competition even started. First, we tried to team up, but it turns out that's against competition rules.

"You guys have nothing to worry about," I tell them. "No matter whose cake wins, we're still opening Jessy's Macaroons."

Rune grins. "You named our bakery?"

I grin back and place a finger against his lips. "Shush, you. No talking."

"Jessy's right, before we both shift." Mac grins. "Now, go out there, you two, and win that prize."

Sienna leads Bax and me onto the stage and has us stand on either side of her while she talks about the sponsors.

"And now for the winner of the Epic Bake-Off." She finally gets to the good part, and my heart races in anticipation.

Logically, I know, win or lose, nothing will change, but I still have to know. I gave this competition my all, and I took an enormous risk with my non-traditional cake. The question is, did it pay off?

Sienna clears her throat dramatically. “This year, it was a very close competition, and the judges could not decide on a winner.”

A few people in the live studio audience gasp. I spot Mac and Rune in the front row, and they both grin.

“But,” Sienna adds, “there can only be one winner, and that’s why the prize tonight goes to the cake the judges could not stop talking about.”

I hold my breath. Were they talking about how different my cake was, or how perfect Bax’s cake turned out?

“So, without further ado, tonight’s winner is…”

My heart leaps. My palms start to sweat. Seconds tick by as everyone in the room waits with bated breath.

“Jessy Alexander from Jessy Bakes for her unique twist on a well-loved summer cake.”

I let out a whoop, and everyone starts to cheer. For a split second, I worry the guys might be disappointed about losing, but then Bax scoops me up in his arms and swings me around and around.

Rune and Mac rush up onto the stage and surround us. They wrap me in their arms in a group hug, and then they take turns kissing me.

At the back of my mind, I'm aware that there's an entire studio audience watching and that the event is being live-streamed, but I don't care. All that matters is that I'm here with my pastry shifters... and I just won the Epic Bake-Off.

***

Thank you for reading HER PASTRY SHIFTERS. I hope you loved spending time with Jessy and her pastry shifter mates. Want more delicious shifters with plenty of steam? You're going to love HER DONUT SHIFTERS:

I hate donuts. Can three donut shifters change my mind?

When a donut shop opens down the street from my house, I want it gone. Then I meet the three delicious owners and fall in love at first sight. There's just one problem—they shift into the one thing I hate most: donuts.

Can my three fated mates, a few dozen sugary treats, and a little bit of magic help us set aside our differences and find our happily ever after?

One-click to read HER DONUT SHIFTERS by Mia Harlan today. Or support Mia on Patreon (patreon.com/miaverse) and receive a free copy.

You're also going to love Xavi, the ice block shifter, in **WYNTER**. *In Silver Springs, everyone knows* *your name... and your business. I'm Zoe Wynter, the best magical maid in town, and rumor has it a pair of magical skates is about to help me find my fated mates.* **One-click WYNTER today.**

If you loved Her Pastry Shifters, you'll also love **AMBER**. *I'm in love with my best friend. But one sip of a spelled latte, and two shifters claim I'm their mate.* **One-click AMBER now.**

Sign up for Mia Harlan's **newsletter** for new release announcements and sneak peeks of future books! You can also come hang out with Mia Harlan in her **Facebook group, Harlan's Harem.**

To get early access to all of Mia's books, exclusive bonus scenes, signed annotated paperbacks, custom scenes written just for you, and the opportunity to get to know Mia, support her on Patreon: **patreon.com/miaverse**

***

Thank you for reading. If you enjoyed Her Pastry Shifters, I would really appreciate it if you could leave a review!

Also By Mia Harlan

Shifter Bay Reading Order

Enter a world like no other, and fall in love at first sight with unique, quirky shifters.

Her Donut Shifters

Her Pastry Shifters

Rubber Duckie Shifter Next Door (coming soon)

Silver Springs Reading Order

Lose yourself in a quirky, paranormal small town filled with magic and fated mates.

Amber

Amber: Deja Brew

Amber Goes Yeti

Amber's Christmas Surprise

Violet

Deflated (with Eva Delaney)

Wynter

Moonlit Nephrite (with Eva Delaney)

Tall, Dark, and Haunted (with Hanleigh Bradley)

Saturn (with Hanleigh Bradley)

Venus (with Hanleigh Bradley)

Neptune (with Hanleigh Bradley)

Other

An Espresso Machine's Guide to Love and Mischief (with Eva Delaney)

Glow Sticks (with Sapphire Winters)

Paranormal Reverse Harem Romance Reader Challenge: A Coloring Book

Exclusively on Patreon

These stories are updated regularly as I write them. You'll find them on patreon.com/miaverse

Alpha's Luna

Fractured Heart

Wolf Trapped (with Emilia Rose)

About Mia Harlan

Mia is a USA Today & International Bestselling Author who writes quirky romance guaranteed to make you laugh.

A librarian by day and author by night, she lives in Canada with her husband (who's definitely NOT a vampire) and their Mini Mortal (who doesn't have fangs).

Sign up for Mia's Patreon for exclusive content and early access to future books: **patreon.com/miaverse**

Printed in Great Britain
by Amazon

13852159R10036